T5-AQQ-650

Far Away
Across the Sea

Far Away Across the Sea

STORIES BY

Toon Tellegen

ILLUSTRATED BY

Jessica Ahlberg

TRANSLATED BY

Martin Cleaver

BOXER BOOKS

Introduction

Toon Tellegen first began to invent animal stories to tell his daughter at bedtime. Then, when his daughter grew older, he decided to write them down. He created a world where there is only one forest, one river, one ocean, and one oak tree; a world of imagination where anything is possible. Toon has been

writing stories about the squirrel,
the ant, and the other animals in
the forest for over 25 years, and
to date more than 500 of them
have been published in his native
Holland. His work has been
translated into many different
languages and enjoyed by children
all over the world.

Contents

Reflection

Sometimes the squirrel looked in the mirror beside his door and didn't know what to think of himself. He stared at his ears and his nose and at the wrinkles on his forehead, but he always saw the same thing and never knew what to think of it.

"I want to ask you something," he said to himself.

"Fire away," he answered.

"If only I knew what," he said.

He gazed at himself for a long time. Then suddenly he said, "Maybe I should write to you."

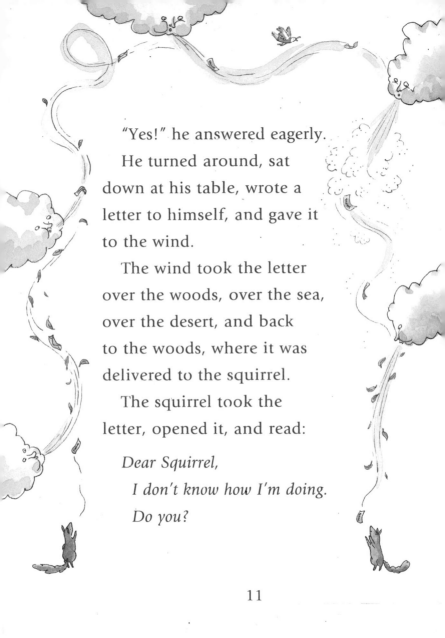

"Yes!" he answered eagerly.

He turned around, sat down at his table, wrote a letter to himself, and gave it to the wind.

The wind took the letter over the woods, over the sea, over the desert, and back to the woods, where it was delivered to the squirrel.

The squirrel took the letter, opened it, and read:

Dear Squirrel,
I don't know how I'm doing.
Do you?

11

The squirrel looked
at the letter, then sat down in
front of the window.

It was a beautiful day. The sun
was high in the sky, and its light
shone down on all the trees, all
the leaves, and all the branches.
There were a few small, elegant
white clouds in the sky, and no
wind blew. The squirrel breathed
in deeply and smelled the summer
scents of the woods. He waved

12

to the swan flying up above, and
to the caterpillar who was crawling
slowly down a branch of the
beech tree.

The squirrel sat there for a long
time. Then he wrote another letter
to himself. The wind rose and took
the letter over the woods, over the
sea, over the desert, and delivered
it back to the squirrel as the sun
was setting.

He opened it quickly and read:

Dear Squirrel,

I don't know either. But if you go outside later and sit at the very end of the large branch, I'll say something to you. I . . .

The squirrel carefully folded up the letter and put it away in the bottom drawer of his cupboard.

The mirror was hanging on the wall above it, but it was dark and he could not make out his own reflection. He went outside to sit on the very end of the large branch to hear what he had to say. His heart thumped.

"Shh," he said.

The Mountain

One day, the pike swam upstream until he reached the waterfall. "This won't be easy," he thought. He pulled himself together and swam forward at full speed. At first he managed to make some progress, but after a while he felt tired and began to swim slower and slower. By the time he'd gotten halfway up the waterfall, he'd had enough. He yawned and fell asleep.

When he woke up the next morning, he tried to swim on, but he still felt tired and made no progress.

The elephant, who was strolling along the riverbank, heard him sigh.

"Do you need some help?" he
inquired. He walked over to the
waterfall, sucked up the pike
with his trunk, and spat
him out a little way
upstream. The pike fell into
the river with a splash. "Now
I'm even farther from home,"
he moaned.

"Where do you want
to go?" the elephant asked.

"That way," said the pike,
pointing with his
tail fin to the top
of the mountain.

"Oh, that's not
too far," said
the elephant.

19

He picked up the pike again
and swung him up toward
the top of the mountain. But
the elephant had underestimated
his own strength. The pike flew
over the mountain and landed in
a cloud. The wind rose and blew
the cloud back across the sky to
just above the river. Then it
started to rain, and the pike fell
back into the water.

"This is awful!" he cried.

The elephant stood under
a bush nearby, sheltering from the
rain. When he heard the pike's cries
he ran over and asked what it had

been like up on the mountain.

"I haven't been there," said the pike.

"You haven't?" said the elephant. "But you still want to go there?"

"Yes, of course," said the pike.

The elephant lifted him up, very cautiously this time, and threw him gently toward the mountain. It wasn't much of a throw, and the pike only got as far as the poplar tree that stood beside the river.

The starling, who lived in the poplar tree, was sitting in his chair, lamenting.

"If only I knew what I was good for," he said.

21

"You'd better ask the elephant,"
said the pike, as he flew through
the roof and landed on the floor
in front of the starling's chair.

"Aha, Pike," said the starling
as he flapped his wings together.
"You've dropped in unexpectedly!"

The pike gasped for breath and
asked if he could use the bathtub.

Once the pike was settled
in the tub, the starling
offered him
a cup of tea.

"I've never drunk tea before," said the pike.

As the evening passed, the pike forgot where he had been going and the starling forgot to wonder what he was good for. They had many things to tell one another and agreed to visit each other more often.

"Your place or mine," said the starling.

"From time to time," said the pike.

"Sometime around late morning," said the starling.

"Or in the afternoon," said the pike. "The afternoon is fine too."

The Mussel's

Party

One night, when the squirrel was fast asleep, the wind blew a letter under his front door. He heard the paper rustling, jumped out of bed, and opened the letter. It was a small, gray note that smelled a little sour.

The squirrel read:

Dear Squirrel,

I would be honored if you would come to my party. It will be a very modest party. I'm not inviting anyone else. Will you come right away?

Mussel

The squirrel got dressed quickly,
grabbed a jar of pickled beechnuts,
and hurried to the
beach as fast as
he could.

The mussel
lived in an inlet.
The squirrel
knocked on his shell.

"Shh," a voice whispered
from inside.

"It's me," said the squirrel
softly, "the squirrel."

The mussel opened his shell
ever so slightly and looked out
at the squirrel. "Oh," he said.

"Happy birthday," said the squirrel.

"I have something for you." He held
out the jar of beechnuts.

"Put it down over there,"
said the mussel.

The squirrel sat down. The warm
seawater swirled around his bushy
tail, and the mussel drifted back
and forth in front of him.

It was quiet for a long time. Then the mussel said, "Do you think this is a nice party?"

"Yes, of course," said the squirrel.

"You know," said the mussel, "you should always laugh at parties."

"Yes," said the squirrel.

They fell silent again. After a long time, the mussel took a piece of licorice root from under his shell.

"Here is something tasty for you," he said, offering it to the squirrel.

The squirrel began to chew. "Delicious," he said.

After a while, the mussel spoke again. "It's not my birthday," he said.

"Isn't it?" replied the squirrel.

"No," said the mussel. "I never celebrate my birthday. You always have to do so much preparing."

"Yes," said the squirrel.

"This is just a party."

"Oh."

They sat in silence for a long time. The mussel gazed at the squirrel, and the squirrel felt the reflections of the sun's rays in the water shine on his face.

"Is this fun enough?" he asked.

The mussel nodded.

As evening approached, the mussel said, "Now you have to go. Bye." He closed his shell and drifted away.

"Thank you," said the squirrel, but the mussel couldn't hear him.

Slowly and contentedly, the squirrel waded to the beach and strolled back toward the woods.

Practice

"*I*," the snail said to
the ant one day, "am going
to keep practicing for
as long as it takes until I
can run faster than you."
"Well," said the ant,
looking at the snail,
"you really should
start right away."
"Yes," said the snail, and
he withdrew into a bush,
marked out a track, and
started practicing. The ant
heard him puffing
and panting as
he worked.

34

The ant strolled on through
the woods and decided to stop for
a nap on the bank of the river.
"Who knows what
I'll dream about today,"
he thought.

Soon he had
fallen into a deep sleep and was
dreaming about a number so small,
it was even smaller than one.

As he walked back home that
evening thinking about the number,
the snail called out to him. "Ant!"

"Yes" said the ant, and he saw
the snail emerging from the bushes.

"The time has come," said the snail.

"I beg your pardon?" said the ant
in surprise.

"I can run faster than you."

The ant remembered their
conversation that morning.
He sighed.

But the snail had already drawn
a starting line and said, "To the
river." He counted to three. Then,
to his amazement, the ant saw the
snail shoot off at great speed
and disappear between
the trees.

He started running as fast
as he could, following the
snail's thin, slimy trail.

When, gasping for breath, the ant

finally reached the river, he found
that the snail had already crossed
the finish line. He sat there, calmly
polishing his shell.

"I won," he said.

The ant didn't reply. He clamped his jaw shut and looked the other way, hoping that the squirrel hadn't seen him lose the race.

"Tomorrow I'm going to fly," said the snail. "Of course, I'll need to practice first."

The ant walked home. That night he slept badly. The next day he caught himself peering up at the sky. "He'll never be able to fly," he said to himself. "Never! It's quite impossible!"

But late that afternoon,
the snail came past, fluttering
slowly and clumsily.
He swerved, bumped into
blades of grass, and
sometimes veered
perilously to one side,
but he was flying.

When he saw
the ant, he waved
and called,
"Do come and fly. It's
not that difficult at all.
You only have to take off."
The ant looked at the
ground and kicked a loose
root as hard as he could.

A Secret Encounter

The squirrel was walking through
the woods one day when he bumped
into the elephant.

"Which of us wasn't looking where
we were going?" the elephant asked.
A bump was appearing on his head.

"I saw you walking along,"
said the squirrel.

"Then it must be my fault,"
said the elephant.

The squirrel's nose felt sore, and
he prodded it cautiously. He and the
elephant sat down together in the
grass under the oak tree.

"Where were you going?" asked the elephant.

"I don't know," said the squirrel. "I was just thinking about that."

The elephant cleared his throat, threw back his ears, and said, "I was on my way to a secret encounter."

"A secret encounter?" the squirrel asked in surprise.

"Yes," said the elephant. "A secret encounter."

"Who with?" asked the squirrel.

"Ah," said the elephant. "If I told you that, then it wouldn't be a secret encounter anymore, would it?"

"What are you going to do at this secret encounter?" asked the squirrel.

"I see what you're doing," said the elephant, smiling broadly. "You're trying to trick me! But I won't fall for it. My encounter's secret and that's all I'm going to say."

"Good," said the squirrel. "That's fine by me. By the way, I think I know . . ."

"What do you know?" asked the elephant, looking worried.

"Ah . . ." said the squirrel, studying the tip of his tail. "That would be telling."

The elephant gave a loud laugh.

"Oh, Squirrel," he said, "you're so predictable. You're just trying to trick me again. The beetle already warned me about—" He fell silent, and a black look crossed his face. The squirrel continued to gaze at the tip of his tail.

"I have a secret encounter with someone else," said the elephant. "Not the beetle. Do you understand?"

"Yes," said the squirrel.

"Do you swear?"

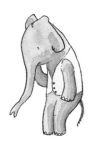

The squirrel thought for a moment, then said, "Yes. You have a secret encounter with someone else. Not the beetle."

"Let's just say, for the sake of
argument, that it's with the snail,"
said the elephant.

"Yes," replied the squirrel. "Let's
say that."

The elephant sat there looking
dejected. His gray back was more
crooked than usual, and there
were at least a hundred
wrinkles in his trunk.

"What kind of
secret encounter are
you having with the snail?"

"No," said the elephant. "You'll
never get that out of me. Never."

The squirrel and the elephant
sat in silence under the oak tree for
a long time. The sun shone down

through the leaves and the dust
appeared to dance in the air above
the bushes. The butterfly sat on a
nearby branch, apparently deep in
thought. The falcon soared through
the sky high above, heading toward
the meadow beyond the woods.

"Squirrel?"
said the elephant.

"Yes?"
said the squirrel.

"Can you keep a secret?"

"Of course," said the squirrel,
trying to remember which secret he
had been keeping recently. It seemed
to him that the elephant was very
worried about something.
His forehead sunk over his eyes and

his trunk looked as if it were made of wax.

"A secret doesn't weigh anything," said the squirrel. "You don't have to hide it, and if you forget it, you're keeping it really well."

"If you forget it, it's not a secret anymore!" exclaimed the elephant.

"Of course it is," said the squirrel. "What else would it be?"

"It would be nothing," said the elephant very softly, "and that's awful."

The elephant's thoughts were all tangled up. Suddenly he felt as if something cracked and tore his head apart. No matter how hard he thought about it, he couldn't remember the secret that he had planned to discuss with the beetle at their secret meeting.

"It's gone," he mumbled. He stood up, wobbled for a moment, and said, "Well, I've got to go."

There were so many wrinkles in his forehead that he couldn't keep his eyes open. The woods echoed with the sound of him crashing into trees. Then there was a loud splash.

"That must be the river," thought the squirrel.

The Spoonbill's Birthday

The spoonbill's birthday was the biggest celebration that the woods had ever seen, though no one really knew why. There was more honey and oak juice and nut drink than at any ordinary birthday. The spoonbill sat at the head of the table, filling plates and bowls and cups. Each new course was greeted by cries of "Ah!" and "Oh!" and "Yum!"

It was a warm summer's evening, and the half-moon cast a soft light

across the clearing where the party
was taking place.

Everyone sat next to their favorite
neighbor, and everything tasted
wonderful.

When everyone was half full, the
spoonbill tapped his plate.

"Friends," he said.

Slowly the chewing and slurping
stopped.

"Tonight we have a special
performance," he continued.

"It is a performance without words. The beetle will dance with the ant."

"That isn't a performance," said the bream from his water bowl.

"Ah, but they won't just dance," said the spoonbill. "They will move us."

"Move us?" said the frog. "Does that mean we can't move ourselves? Ha ha ha!"

No one laughed, and the frog fell silent, feeling embarrassed.

The glowworm extinguished his light, and there, on a platform under the oak tree, which was illuminated by the light of the firefly, the beetle and the ant suddenly appeared.

They seemed to gleam in a way

that no one had ever seen before. The beetle was dressed entirely in black, while the ant had occasional spots of white on his costume – spots that shimmered in the light.

"Oh," everyone gasped.

The clearing fell silent, and the nightingale, who was standing in the bush beside the oak tree, began to sing. The beetle threw his arm around the ant's waist, and they floated across the platform.

The two animals danced more beautifully than anyone had ever danced before. The spoonbill's guests were moved, and many tears were shed.

The squirrel was most moved, because as he danced, the ant occasionally glanced across at him. He thought about a journey they were going to make together and how wonderful it would be, and, though he did not know why, he felt tears rolling down his cheeks.

They danced for a long time, the beetle and the ant. When the nightingale finally sang his last note, they stood still.

No one moved or said anything or clapped. Then, after a long pause, the spoonbill whispered, "Were you moved?"

Everyone nodded, even the frog, who had turned white with emotion. The bream was swimming in his own tears. The beetle's eyes sparkled, and the ant nodded and pursed his lips in a strange way.

Then the spoonbill produced a cake that was so light you couldn't see it or taste it.

"What a pity," said the bear.

But the other animals said, "Wow," and vowed never to forget the spoonbill's birthday.

The Flood

One day it rained so hard that the river broke its banks. The water rose and rose, and before long most of the trees in the forest had water halfway up their trunks.

The carp didn't mind the rain. He swam out of the river and through the woods, and knocked on the squirrel's door. The squirrel was standing on his table.

"Come in,"
he called with a
nervous voice.

"Hello, Squirrel!" said the
carp, and he swam inside.

"Take a seat," said the squirrel.
The table he was standing on
disappeared under the water. The
carp settled himself comfortably by
the window. He admired the dark
green view and waved at the pike,
who was swimming along in the
distance.

"Would you like some tea?"
asked the squirrel.

"Yes, please," said the carp.

The squirrel scattered some tea

leaves in the corner of the room
and stirred the water with his tail.
"I'm afraid it will be rather weak,"
he told the carp.

"Oh, that doesn't matter," said
the carp, who was in a very good
mood. He swam to the corner and
took a couple of sips of the tea that
was splashing around there.

"You know," he said. "I wish it
rained all the time. And I wish the
moon would shine underwater
for a change."

"Oh, really?" said the squirrel as
he climbed onto the vase that stood
in the middle of his table.

"I don't like the air," said the carp.

"I don't trust it. I think it's sneaky."

"But that can't be true," said the squirrel. "I love the air!" Small waves rippled around his shoulders.

There was a tap on the window.

"The salmon!" cried the carp. He opened the window and the salmon swam inside. The squirrel dived off the vase and swam outside. He climbed onto a branch above his house. The rain continued to fall.

After a while, the ant swam up to the beech tree. He looked just as wet and sorry for himself as the squirrel did. They sat side by side on the branch in silence. Below

them, in the squirrel's house, it was
getting busy. The perch and the
dolphin had dropped in, followed
by the bream and the stickleback.

"There's plenty of tea," called the
squirrel.

The bubbles of air floating up
told them that the guests were
dancing and singing.

Then the moon came up and,
with a gentle splash, the last drop
of rain fell into the gleaming water.

The stars began to twinkle, and
very cautiously, the squirrel and
the ant fell asleep.

The Mosquito's Hat

On the grasshopper's birthday, the mosquito sang a song and wore a hat that he took off and ate during the performance. When the hat was finished, so was the song. It had been a sad song, and occasionally someone had sighed or wiped a tear from his cheek.

"Thank you very much, Mosquito," said the grasshopper.

"Let's have more to eat!" said
the bear.

"Yes!" everyone shouted.

A loud shuffling and snorting
was heard as everyone filled their
plates again.

The mosquito sat down in a
corner.

"Why," he wondered,
"did I eat my hat?"

It was the only one he had, and he always got a headache if he flew without it when it was cold.

"Now I'll have to stay inside all winter," he thought sadly. "And I have a bellyache too. I'll never sing again."

He sat there for some time, thinking. All the other animals were concentrating on their plates and had forgotten all about him. Only the butterfly came over to speak to him.

"That was such a beautiful song!" he said, putting his wing around the mosquito.

"Oh," said the mosquito, "if only I hadn't sung it. Now my hat is gone."

"But if you hadn't eaten it, the sorrow of which you sang would have broken you," said the butterfly.

The mosquito gave him a surprised look.

"Yes," the butterfly continued. "I'm often broken with sorrow at something I said or dreamed or thought."

"And if you'd eaten something at the time . . ."

"Exactly," said the butterfly. "But I can't eat anymore."

"You're not still broken now, are you?" asked the mosquito.

"Not visibly," said the butterfly softly.

"Oh," said the mosquito.

"I have a hat for you at home," said the butterfly, "made of moss. It's exactly your size."

"Oh, thank you," said the mosquito, and he began zooming around cheerfully. Suddenly he felt a little hungry.

"Shall I get you something sweet to eat?" he asked the butterfly.

The butterfly shook his head, and just briefly, the mosquito thought he could see a crack running right through him.

"Drop by tomorrow," said
the butterfly. Then he flew away
in large, round loops.
The mosquito sat down at
a table and poured himself a
glass of dark red juice.
"Lovely song, Mosquito,"
said the squirrel.
"What does hat taste like?"
asked the bear through
a mouthful of cake.
"Musty," said the mosquito.

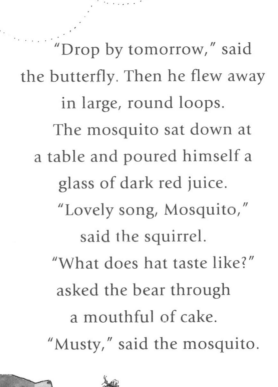

A Distant Corner
of the Woods

One day, the ant and the squirrel walked farther than they had ever walked before. They waded through unknown scrubland and untrodden bushes. They chatted for a long time, but after a while they had nothing more to say, and so they fell silent.

Under an old tree, in a bleak and distant corner of the woods, they came across the mammoth.

"Who's that?"
whispered the squirrel.

"The mammoth," whispered
the ant, who knew the names of
all the animals, even the ones
that didn't exist.

"I've never heard of him," said the squirrel.

"No," said the ant.

The mammoth was chewing on a piece of grass. He gazed at the two animals with tired eyes. "Who are you?" he asked.

"I'm the ant," said the ant. "And this is the squirrel."

"Oh, it doesn't really matter anyway," said the mammoth. "I don't know anyone."

"No one?" asked the squirrel.

"No one," said the mammoth.

"Not even the fly?"

"The fly? No."

"Or the elephant?"

"The elephant?
Never heard of him."

The mammoth yawned.

"Are you feeling sleepy?" asked
the ant.

"I've never felt sleepy," said the
mammoth. "How do you get to feel
that?"

The ant and the squirrel
remained silent. Then the ant said,
"May I ask, when's your birthday?"

"I don't think I have a birthday," said the mammoth.

"What do you celebrate, then?" asked the squirrel in amazement.

"Nothing," he replied.

The mammoth's coat was thin and full of holes, and his trunk looked tired and cumbersome. His eyes traveled slowly from the squirrel to the ant and back again. The squirrel suggested that they all celebrate something together, but the mammoth shook his head.

"We have plenty of time," said the squirrel.

"I don't," said the mammoth. "I don't have any time at all."

He went back to chewing on his piece of grass. He didn't seem to be able to see the squirrel and the ant anymore.

They left him there and walked back into the woods.

"Do you think we could help him find a little time?" asked the squirrel.

"No," said the ant. "Our time doesn't fit him."

"Too big?" asked the squirrel.

"Too small," said the ant.

Far Away
Across the Sea

One morning, the wind blew a letter under the squirrel's front door. The envelope was blue and smelled of salt, as if it had traveled from far away, across the sea.

The squirrel opened the letter and read:

Squirrel,

I wish you all the best with what you read here. I hope that it touches you and, who knows, that it might even make you weep with tears of happiness. Don't write back to me, but enjoy my words and hope fervently you'll get more such letters.

Your humble bird of paradise

85

The next day, the squirrel received a letter in a red envelope. It smelled of palm and reeds.

Squirrel,

What did you think of my last letter? Beautiful, eh? And this one is even more beautiful. This letter will make you quiver with happiness. Do you ever quiver with happiness? Or do you do something else with happiness? Beam? Glow? If you glow, then you should be glowing now.

Your insignificant bird of paradise

The following day, another letter arrived. It was a yellow letter that smelled of pine and wild tea.

Squirrel,

The letter you'll
receive tomorrow . . .
Oh, that letter . . .

Your most unfindable bird
of paradise

The next morning, the squirrel woke up early. He sat by his front door and listened to the wind, hoping that it just might deliver another letter.

A Line

"This far. And no farther," the squirrel said to himself. He drew a line in the sand on the riverbank and stood on one side of it.

Long ago, he had resolved to draw such a line and then not to cross it.

"Then I'll know where I stand," he thought. He felt tired, so he sat down. The sun set slowly, and silence and peace descended upon the woods and the river. Occasionally the scent of resin or heather wafted past on the breeze.

90

The squirrel rested his head in his hands and looked over to the other side of the line. It was as if everything was different there, but he couldn't quite decide how

Suddenly he heard a call: "Squirrel! Squirrel!"

He recognized the cricket's voice.

"Yes," he replied.

"Come over here," called the cricket.

"Where are you?"

"I'm here."

The squirrel looked around and saw something move in the bushes.

"Ah," he said. "I can't come over to you. You're on the wrong side of the line."

"Then I'll have to eat it on my own," said the cricket.

The squirrel leaned right across the line, trying to see what the cricket was talking about. He could only just make out the end of the cricket's tail, but he caught a whiff of a familiar scent.

"Wait a second!" he cried. He looked around to make sure no one could see him, then quickly rubbed out the line with his tail. "Maybe it's not such a good idea at all to know where you stand," he thought.

"I'm coming!" he called.

But when he reached the bush,

the cricket said, "Where were you? I've eaten it all on my own now."

"What?" asked the squirrel.

"The . . . umm . . . what do you call a thing like that?"

"A beechnut?"

"Yes! Indeed. A beechnut. All gone. I can't really say I enjoyed it," said the cricket with a shrug of his shoulders.

The squirrel hung his head and shuffled home in the twilight. As he walked, he made up his mind never to draw a line again. "And if I ever say 'here and no farther' again," he thought, "then I'll have to shake my head right away. Promise?"

He nodded, and made that promise to himself.

The Right Note

$\mathcal{A}$t the cricket's party, all
the guests wore green jackets and
red caps.

The thrush was planning to sing
a song at the party. He'd practiced
for a long time, but when he stood
there in front of the sea
of green and red, he
felt nervous, and
his heart throbbed
in his throat.

The cricket nodded, and the thrush began.

He sang a note and then stopped, because it wasn't the right note. He tried another note and then another, but none of them was the right one. "I can't find the right note," he admitted at last, feeling dejected. The animals fell silent for a moment, then started talking all at once.

"It's gone."

"What's gone?"

"The note!"

"Maybe it's behind him!"

"Did he leave it at home?"

"Why isn't he wearing a red cap?"

Questions, questions, but no answers. The squirrel and the ant, who were sitting side by side, shook their heads.

"It can't have just disappeared," said the ant.

"Might it be the E?" called the squirrel.

"No," said the thrush.

The elephant asked if it was the G, the grasshopper recited a series of poems, and the lark sang a song.

"Was it one of those notes?" he asked when the song was finished.

"No," said the thrush.

The first note of the thrush's song was nowhere to be found. And without this, the cricket explained, the party couldn't go on. "Alas," he said, "you must all go home."

The animals walked home, grumbling and hungry. Only the thrush stayed behind, crying bitter tears. The cricket patted him on the shoulder and said, "Never mind.

I expect it happens all the time."

It grew cold and the cricket
went to bed. The thrush remained
outside, crouching on a twig,
allowing his thoughts to roam
wherever they wanted.

As the sun rose, the thrush suddenly
found the note that he had
been searching for.

It appeared
unexpectedly,
as if it had fallen
from the sky. He
immediately broke into
his song; a song that was more
warm and beautiful than any other.

Only the glowworm, who often
stayed up at night, thinking by the
light of his own glow, heard him.
The song moved him so much
that a tear fell from his eye and
extinguished his light. Then, quite
suddenly, he fell asleep. Then there
was no one else to hear the thrush,
jubilant and triumphant, singing
on a dark twig.

Wet

One day, the squirrel was
sitting on the end of a branch,
deep in thought, when suddenly
he fell off. Then a gust of wind
picked him up and blew him
into the pond. There he
disappeared under the water,
only to emerge again a
moment later.

"Help!" he cried.

The carp stuck his head
up beside him.

"I'm soaking wet!" said
the squirrel.

"Wet, wet . . ." said the carp.
"Watch out you don't get dry."

"But if I'm wet, I get cold,"

said the squirrel, and he started shivering demonstratively.

"When I get dry, I feel hot," said the carp, and he lowered his head below the water. Only his lips remained above the surface. "Sometimes," he continued, "the air rains down here . . . Fat drops of air fall around me, and then I start to boil. Recently the rain dried me out for three whole days. I had to go and lie under the weeds. No, it's better never to get dry . . ."

"But what's dry for you, for me is—" began the squirrel, but the carp had already disappeared into the depths.

"I shouldn't always act as if I know it all," thought the squirrel. "Maybe I'm wrong. Maybe I'm always wrong." He shivered. "Who knows," he thought, "maybe I'm feeling warm now."

As he swam back toward the bank he thought, "Maybe I'm flying high in the sky, wearing a green jacket . . ."

He lay down on the bank in the sun and thought, "Maybe I don't know anything. That would be strange, wouldn't it?" He frowned, and a few drops of water appeared from the wrinkles on his forehead and rolled down his cheeks.

Then he fell asleep.

A little while later, the carp stuck his head up again, looked around, and saw the squirrel lying in the grass. He shook his head, swam to the bank, and very carefully used his tail to splash a wave of water over the squirrel. "You'll get dry," he said softly.

The squirrel dreamed that he was feeling very warm and that sweat was pouring from him, while his fingers, his ears, and his nose turned blue and white.

Someone's Birthday

"*T*his honey is delicious," said the ant.

"This honey is awful," said the bumblebee.

They sat at a long table among the other animals. It was someone's birthday, someone else had just made a speech, and now, at last, they could tuck in.

The ant took another bite and said, "No, you're right. This honey is awful."

The bumblebee also took another bite and said, "No, *you're* right. This honey is delicious."

"Rubbish," said the ant. "I'm not right at all. You're right."

"Absolutely not," said the bumblebee. "You're right. I am most certainly not right, whichever way you look at it."

"Oh, you'd like that, wouldn't you?" said the ant. "But it isn't that easy. You . . . are . . . right."

The bumblebee turned and gave the ant a shove. "You're right," he cried. "So there!"

The ant scrambled to his feet and tugged at the bumblebee's left wing. The bumblebee twisted one of the ant's antennae, and the ant grabbed the bumblebee around the waist and squeezed as hard as he could.

"Ouch!" they both cried. "But you're right."

The bumblebee grabbed the tablecloth, and the other animals watched as their delicacies began to slide down the table and tumble onto the ground.

"I . . . am . . . not . . . right!" shouted the ant.

"Yes . . . you . . . are!" cried the bumblebee, buzzing wildly. He pushed the ant under the table with all his might. "Lovely party," muttered the bear, who had only been able to save his spoon from falling to the floor, while the carp looked at the empty water around him, feeling disappointed.

Under the table, the bumblebee and the ant continued their fight. Neither of them wanted to admit how right they were, no matter how many legs were bent or how many antennae were bruised.

The other animals went home somber and hungry. The ground was covered with delicious leftovers, but no one could remember who had been celebrating what.

Late that night, the ant and the bumblebee lay exhausted side by side on the ground. With his last ounce of energy, the bumblebee put one of his wings over the ant.

"You must be cold," he said.

"No, I'm very hot!" said the ant, who was still feeling angry.

"You're right," said the bumblebee, but he left his wing there.

The ant didn't say anything, but he put his only uninjured arm over the bumblebee. He waited until the bumblebee fell asleep. Then, in a very soft voice, he said, "You too."

Everything
Was Different

One morning everything looked different. The squirrel looked out of his window and saw that the sky was green. He rubbed his eyes, looked again, but the sky was still green, and the tree opposite his house was white and glistened as if it was made of glass.

He dressed quickly, noticing that he now had six feet instead of two and a very tiny tail. He climbed down the beech tree and ran to see the ant.

"Ant! Ant!" he called.

"Yes," a voice said from behind the door. It was a dark voice, and when the door opened the ant

stood there with two trunks instead of a mouth and only one eye, which sat slightly to one side, just under his chin. His nose was yellow, and the rest of his body was pink with the occasional bright red patch.

"What's the matter with you?" asked the squirrel.

The ant shrugged. One of his shoulders rose all the way up to the ceiling, while the other hardly moved. "I don't know," he said in the same low-pitched voice.

"Come and look outside," said the squirrel.

The squirrel and the ant walked through the woods and found

that everything was different. The moss was yellow and the path went straight up and ended in a cloud that was red and smelled of straw. The river flowed beside its bed and the carp strolled along the bank on thin red legs.

"Who could possibly be responsible for this?" the squirrel asked.

He and the ant considered everyone they knew. They thought about the lizard and the hummingbird, rejected the spider, excluded the beetle, and still couldn't decide who was to blame.

That afternoon, the ant felt like

eating some tree root, which was
something he'd never felt like
before. Several trees were standing
upside down, so it didn't take him
long to find a tasty-looking root.
He took a bite and thought of
things he'd never thought of before:
shoelaces, gnarls, and broken
feathers.

That afternoon, the squirrel
and the ant bumped into lots of
animals. Everyone looked different,
but not unrecognizable. Even the
elephant with spines, little pink
ears, a beak, and hundreds of short
legs was still the elephant. They
recognized him as he floated down

121

the river on his back, singing a melancholy song.

By the evening, everyone had grown quite accustomed to the changes. The ant put his trunks around a willow root and chewed noisily while the squirrel talked about a walk beneath the sea that he had never taken.

The moon appeared above the woods, blue and elongated, and the whole sky glistened, except for the stars, which hung like black spots in the air.

That night, everyone dreamed the strangest things. The squirrel dreamed he had two feet and an enormous tail, while the ant imagined that he was licking a sugar puff and enjoying it. The stickleback dreamed he could swim.

"How lovely," he thought. "I'm swimming!"

"Quiet!" said the mole, who was lying next to him at the top of the poplar tree. He dreamed he dug tunnels under the ground. "Maybe I'm on my way to something tasty," he dreamed in surprise.

The Depth of Sleep

The squirrel and the sparrow strolled through the woods at a leisurely pace. As they walked they talked about all the things that came into their minds. The sun was shining, and they didn't have anything they particularly needed to do, or anywhere they particularly needed to go.

The sparrow explained to the squirrel how you could measure the depth of sleep.

"I discovered the method myself," he said, brushing a speck of dust from his wing. "You stand ten steps away from someone who's asleep, and then you say his name at exactly this volume: Hoo!"

"Hoo?" asked the squirrel.

"That's a standard measure," said the sparrow. "If he doesn't wake up, you take one step toward him and you say his name again. You keep going on until he wakes up. The number of steps you've taken is the depth of his sleep."

"I see," said the squirrel.

"Look, the beetle is asleep over there," said the sparrow. They just happened to be passing the beetle, who was lying asleep under the oak tree, snoring gently.

"Just watch this," said the sparrow.

He took ten steps away from the beetle, turned around, and said (just as loudly as he had just said "Hoo"), "Beetle."

Nothing happened. The beetle remained fast asleep. The sparrow came one step closer and, once again, said, "Beetle."

Again, nothing happened.

And he went on, one step at a time, toward the beetle, until he was right beside his ear. "Beetle," he called.

But the beetle slept on.

The sparrow turned to the squirrel and announced, "He is

in an immeasurably deep sleep."

"What's immeasurably?" asked the squirrel.

"Well . . ." said the sparrow, "it is, for example, how warm time is or who most loves the sky or is most birthdayed."

"Oh," said the squirrel.

Something rustled.

"Can't you keep walking and talk farther away?" asked the beetle. "I'm trying to get some sleep."

The sparrow and the squirrel walked on.

"The beetle is a bad example," said the sparrow. "He just keeps on sleeping."

They strolled on in silence for some time.

"It's a good method," said the sparrow.

The squirrel remained silent.
A little while later, they came across the lion, asleep in the grass.

"Aha!" said the sparrow. "Now there's a good sleeper. Just watch this." He took ten paces, turned around, and said, "Lion."

"Yes?" roared the lion, jumping to his feet.

"There you are!" said the sparrow to the squirrel. Then he turned to the lion and said, "You couldn't have been sleeping less deeply."

130

"That's true," replied the lion, giving the sparrow an angry look.

"Well?" said the sparrow, looking satisfied. The squirrel nodded.

They walked on, while the lion roared behind them.

"How on earth will I get back to sleep again now?" he cried.

The sparrow arranged his feathers and said, "I'm working on a new method to measure how deeply someone is thinking." The lion was still roaring in the distance.

"That'll be quite something," said the squirrel.

"Oh," said the sparrow, "you can find out anything at all, if you really want to."

The Tree

"I wish," thought the squirrel, "that I could accidentally fall out of the tree and be terribly shocked."

He shut his eyes and took a couple of steps forward, but he didn't fall.

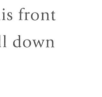

"Oh," he said, "when I want to fall, I can't fall. All these stupid branches get in the way!"

He ran backward and forward a couple more times with his eyes closed, but still he did not fall.

"I give up," he thought. He turned around, opened his front door, and slipped and fell down the tree.

"Ouch," he cried as he landed on the ground.

He heard a buzzing beside him.

"Who's there?" he asked, rubbing the back of his head.

"It's me. Your tree."

"I didn't know you could talk," said the squirrel.

"Neither did I," said the tree. "But I can."

Then the tree pulled its roots out of the ground, folded up its branches, and walked away.

"Hey," called the squirrel. "Where are you going?"

"I don't know," replied the tree.

The squirrel wanted to go after it,

but he had fallen so hard that
his feet were stuck in the ground,
and he couldn't free them.
He watched sadly as his tree
disappeared between the other trees.

The ant found him still sitting
there some time later, feeling
sorrowful. "I can see," he said,
"that you fell."

"My tree's gone," said the
squirrel sadly.

The ant
looked in
amazement at the
place where the beech tree had been
standing.

"It walked away," said the squirrel.

136

"Why?" asked the ant.

"Oh, I don't know. Maybe it was because I said something about its branches."

"Oh," said the ant. He didn't really understand, but he suspected that the tree must have had a pretty good reason to walk away like that.

"We have to go after it," he said. He pulled the squirrel out of the ground and together they walked through the woods, across the river, over the meadow, along the beach, and through the desert, following the trail of the beech tree. At last, deep in the desert, not far from the end of the world, they found it.

"Hello, Tree," said the squirrel, looking in the other direction. The tree nodded.

"I promise I'll never do it again," said the squirrel.

"This isn't the right place for you, Tree," said the ant.

"No." The tree rustled a couple of its dry leaves.

"We always got on so well together, didn't we?" said the squirrel.

"Fairly well," said the tree, peeling a piece of curling bark from its trunk with its longest branch.

"Will you come back?" asked the squirrel. He gave the tree a hand, and the tree gave him a branch.

"Very well then," said the tree.

The squirrel and the tree walked home together. The ant walked close behind them, enjoying the shade. When they reached the woods, the tree went back and stood in its old place.

"I won't say anything at all for a while," buzzed the tree.

The ant went home, and the squirrel climbed up the tree, very slowly and carefully. He resolved never to want to fall again.

Keeping in Touch

One day, the ant said goodbye to the squirrel.

"I'm going to be traveling for quite a long time," he said. "I don't know how long, so I'll say farewell in a way that can last for a long time."

They shook hands five times and embraced in such a way that befits a farewell for a long time.

"You will keep in touch, won't you?" called the squirrel as the ant walked away down the woodland path.

"Yes!" the ant called back.

Soon he disappeared from sight, and the squirrel was left on his own. "What kind of journey will it be?"

144

he thought. He knew that it was difficult to say anything about journeys that had not yet begun

A few days later, the squirrel received a letter.

Dear Squirrel,

I'm really traveling now.
I promised you I would keep in touch.
Next time you read an exclamation mark, I'll get in touch.

Are you reading comfortably?
Look out!

At that moment, the squirrel heard a soft noise. It was the unmistakable sound of the ant whistling.

"Ant!" cried the squirrel in delight. He turned the letter over and over, looked between words, in the envelope, and on the floor, but there was no sign of the ant anywhere.

He started reading again, and when he read the exclamation mark, he heard the same soft whistling. If he looked at the exclamation mark for a long time, he could even just about make out a song that the ant often whistled.

He put the letter back in the envelope and laid it on the table beside his bed.

"The ant must be a very long way away," thought the squirrel. "But he's thinking of me!"

The sun shone, and the squirrel sat on the branch in front of his door. Every now and then he stood up and went inside to read the letter again, and each time he saw the exclamation mark he heard the soft whistling of the ant, who was far away, yet keeping in touch.

The squirrel's eyes glistened as he shook his head and thought, "Ant! Ant!"

A Beautiful Day

*I*t was a beautiful morning in the
woods. The thrush whistled softly
in the bush under the oak tree, and
the carp caused an occasional ripple
in the water of the lake. There
was no wind, and the sun shone
overhead, making drops of dew
glisten here and there. By the river,
the soil seemed to be steaming. It
was a mild, clear morning, but it
was going to be a hot day.

The squirrel got up early and sniffed the scent of resin and lilac on the air. He dangled his feet in the water of the lake and wondered what kind of day could possibly be more beautiful than this one. A day with deep, fresh snow? A day with black clouds in the distance and bolts of lightning so beautiful you wanted to reach out and touch them?

Beside him was a sheet of paper. He wanted to write a letter. He had the feeling there was something he wanted to let someone know, but he didn't know who or what. He picked up his pen and wrote:

Dear

Then he put his pen down again.
He wanted to write to everyone:
the albatross, the whale, the
buffalo, and the shrew. He wanted
to congratulate everyone or invite
them or ask them if they had ever
seen such a beautiful day. But who
should he start with?

He closed his eyes. In his
thoughts, he saw the desert and
began to feel very hot. He lay down
in the shadow under a rock and
fell asleep.

Suddenly he started awake.
A small, almost transparent cloud
had passed in front of the sun.

He immediately knew where he was and picked up his pen. "I'll write to the ant," he thought. "It doesn't matter what."

He read what he'd already written:

Dear Squirrel,

He frowned. Dear Squirrel? Had he written that himself?

Suddenly he knew what he should write next.

You wondered if you'd ever seen such a beautiful day before.
The answer is: no.

Goodbye,
Yourself

"What a strange letter," thought the squirrel, but he sent it anyway.

A gentle breeze delivered the letter back to him a little while later. He quickly opened it and read:

Dear Squirrel,

Thank you for your letter. I wanted to let you know that there are many more days like this to come. Countless days!

Goodbye,

Yourself

The squirrel looked at the sky,
at the wind, at the bushes, at the
water, at his pen, and at his hand.
The thrush remained silent, and the
carp disappeared into the depths.

"What a day," thought the
squirrel, and he closed his eyes.

About the Author

Toon Tellegen is one of Holland's most celebrated writers for both children and adults. He started his literary career as a poet and began writing for children in the mid-1980s. Toon lives in Amsterdam and loves reading, telling stories, and huge, sweet cakes.

About the Illustrator

Jessica Ahlberg studied at Winchester School of Art and has gone on to illustrate several books for children. She likes, among other things, writing letters, looking at maps, reading books, doing home improvement and making cakes. She lives in Brighton, England, and loves walking by the sea and sometimes swimming in it.

$\mathcal{D}$iscover more magical books by Toon Tellegen . . .

That evening, the animals made their gifts for the squirrel. They did so quietly and underwater, or deep in the bushes, or high above the clouds, because they wanted to surprise the squirrel. Everyone made a gift. The world rustled and shook, but very quietly, so that the squirrel, sitting in the dark by his window, thought it was so silent everywhere that he could only hear his heart beating.

Dear Snail,

May I invite you to dance with me on top of your house? Just a few steps? That's what I want most of all. I promise I'll dance very delicately, so we won't fall through your roof.

But of course, you can never be really sure.
The elephant

For Quien
Toon Tellegen

For Jill
Jessica Ahlberg

First American edition published in 2012
by Boxer Books Limited.

First published in Great Britain in 2012
by Boxer Books Limited.
www.boxerbooks.com

Translated by Martin Cleaver

Edited by Frances Elks

Book design by Amelia Edwards

ISBN 978-1-907152-37-5

1 3 5 7 9 10 8 6 4 2

Printed in Italy

All of our papers are sourced from managed forests
and renewable resources.

This book was published with the support of the
Dutch foundation for literature.